Is This Good-bye,

Charlie Brown?

Charles M. Schulz

SAM'S MOVING

Random House • New York

Library of Congress Cataloging in Publication Data:

Schulz, Charles M. Is this good-bye, Charlie Brown? SUMMARY: Charlie and the rest of the gang are very unhappy when Linus and Lucy move away. [1. Moving, Household—Fiction. 2. Friendship—Fiction. 3. Cartoons and comics] I. Title. PZ7.S38877 In 1984 [Fic] 83-17801 ISBN: 0-394-85953-7 (trade); 0-394-95953-1 (lib. bdg.)

Manufactured in the United States of America   1 2 3 4 5 6 7 8 9 0

Oh! It's you, my sweet baboo!

I am not your sweet baboo! Can I please speak to—

Did you call to ask me to go to a movie with you? When a boy wants to take a girl to the movies, he calls her up and he asks her, "Would you like to go to the movies with me?"

Grr....But I didn't call you! I want to speak to your brother.

Well, I'll be glad to go to the movies with you. I'll be ready here at noon. Thank you.

Here, my sweet baboo wants
to talk to you!

Boy, oh boy, my first date!

I have something very important
to tell you, Charlie Brown.

Sure, Linus, come right over.

We're moving away, Charlie Brown. My dad has been
transferred and we're moving away.

You should have told me on the phone. I can take bad news better on the phone. Every time the phone rings, I expect it to be bad news, and I'm ready for it.

Well, anyway, I'm moving away. We'll have to go to a new school and everything.

We have a kid in our class who's been to eight schools. He never knows what's going on. But who am I to talk? I've only been to one school and I still don't know what's going on.

My dad has been transferred. Our family has to move to another town. Keep this picture of me on your piano so you won't forget me.

What if I want to forget you and I turn the picture around?

What are you doing?

My sweet baboo is coming by at noon
and we're going to the movies.

Don't count on it!

I thought we might talk about this move of your family's. I don't know what I'll do without Linus. He's my very best friend, not to mention the fact that he's my second baseman.

I notice you don't mention missing *me*, Charlie Brown! I'm leaving, too, you know!

As a matter of fact, I can't help you. I've sold my practice and you'll have to discuss this with the new doctor.

Good morning, Doctor.

Fifty cents! Are you crazy? I'm not going to pay fifty cents! It's my whole week's allowance! Besides, I'm still hoping that they're not moving away. I'll wait for my old doctor.

I'm waiting for my sweet baboo.
He's coming to take me to a movie.

I'm afraid you're going to
have a long wait. My dad's
been transferred! We're
moving to a new city!

I don't believe it!

This may be my last game, Charlie Brown. I'll probably never see you again.

Unless, of course, we happen to go to the same college. What college do you think you'll be going to, Charlie Brown?

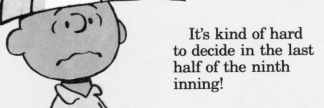

It's kind of hard to decide in the last half of the ninth inning!

We've received an invitation. Linus and Lucy are
having a little farewell lunch. It's being catered.

Lunch? What about my date? What about the movie?!
My sweet baboo was supposed to pick me up at noon! I'm
going to sit here and wait for my date.

Well, have it your way.

Are you sure you got the right caterer?

Not to worry—
Joe Cool came highly
recommended.

By whom, I wonder?

Attention, everybody! Attention! As you know, we are moving to a new city, and this is our way of thanking you all and saying good-bye. Mr. Caterer, serve the lunch!

I propose a farewell toast to Lucy and Linus. Good luck and happiness in your new home!

Hey, I'm not sure, but are these dog biscuits?

What kind of lunch is this?

It must be a fancy continental lunch, sir. I see there's a gravy boat.

It seems to be water, sir!

AAAARGH!

Dog food!! Bleah!! Some lunch! Argh!

Well, I sure hate to say good-bye, Charlie Brown.
It's sure been nice knowing you.

This is really
happening! I can't
believe it!

Snoopy always wanted this blanket.
I think maybe I'll leave it with him.

Linus is gone. If you're still waiting for your sweet baboo, you'd better forget all about it. I just saw him leave. He and Lucy have moved away. Their whole family has just plain moved away.

That's ridiculous! He can't move away! We had a date! Things like this just don't happen! I had a firm date!

We had an understanding!

I'll sue!

See that moving van? Lucy and Linus have moved away.

But I thought she was just kidding! I didn't think they'd really go!

Well, what do you care? You never liked Lucy anyway! You were always picking on her! Go on home and play your ol' Beethoven.

I never even said good-bye.

Look! A postcard from Linus!

"Dear Charlie Brown: This is the motel we stayed in the first night. It had a swimming pool, but we didn't go swimming. Lucy has been crabby all day. I have to ride in the back seat with her. This looks like it's going to be a long trip. Your friend, Linus. P.S. Tell Snoopy to enjoy my blanket!"

I understand you heard from Linus.

Yes, he sent me a postcard from some motel.

It was the saddest postcard I've ever read!

You miss him, huh?

Yep, it's not the same without Linus....

I was gonna challenge your team to a game, but with Lucy and Linus gone it would be a massacre, Chuck!

Now, look here—

Don't say another word, Chuck. I know you're embarrassed for your team, but it's okay. I'll stick to playing in my league—at least they put up a struggle sometimes!

Oh, boy!

Hey, Marcie, we gotta do something about Chuck.
We gotta get his mind on other things.

You're kinda sweet on
Charles, aren't you, sir?

Marcie, are you crazy?

Sweet on Chuck, indeed!
How can I be sweet on a guy
I can strike out with three
pitches!

Marcie, yer crazy!

I guess the only civil thing to do is to call the kid and level with him. I hate to think of him lying there, wide awake, wondering. The poor kid! Maybe I should give him a break...hmmm....

Hello?

This is Patty, Peppermint Patty. How are you, Chuck? I know you haven't been sleeping well, and I wanted to straighten out a few things. So if you wanna come and see me... well, I guess it'll be okay.

Wha…? See you? Wha…?

Yep, if you wanna take me out, oh, say to the movies or somethin'—why, it'll be okay, Chuck.

Okay, kid, thanks for the invitation and the call. No more sleepless nights, eh, Chuck?

It's kind of funny… I never knew ol' wishy-washy Chuck had fallen for me!

What? What am I doing
here? Hello, hello?

I dreamed I spoke to
Peppermint Patty. I must
be going bonkers!

Now I'm wide awake! Good grief, it's one thirty in
the morning! What am I doing up at this unearthly
hour? Maybe I'm dead!

I wonder if I'll ever fall asleep again? Maybe this is it...never to sleep!

Good morning, sir. You're
up early.

I don't know quite how
to put it, Marcie, but I'm
waiting for a date. I was
invited last night, Marcie.
You'll never guess with whom
I had a heart-to-heart talk!

You didn't call and bother
Charles, did you, sir?

What do you mean, bother
Chuck? Last night Chuck
offered to take me to a movie
or something, and I'm waiting
for him.

Well, Marcie, I don't want to be
rude, but two's company and three's
a crowd—get what I mean?

I hope you don't have
to wait too long, sir.

You're not getting much
sleep, are you, Charles?

Last night I felt sure I
was cracking up. I awakened
standing up, holding the phone
to my ear in the middle of the
night!

Did you talk to
Peppermint Patty,
by any chance?

Strange you would say that.
I did dream I had spoken to
Patty on the phone.

Still waiting, sir? I hate to disappoint you, sir, but I saw Charles and he's *not* coming! Charles doesn't even know you called last night. He was asleep!

You're wrong, Marcie. The kid's fallen for me. He said he'd come for me today. You wouldn't understand. You just toodle along. I'll sit here and wait for my date.

If that's the way you want it, sir. Don't stay up all night!

Hello...yes, this is he.

Chuck, someone waited and waited all day. Chuck, someone was stood up! What do you have to say to that? Now someone's feelings are hurt! You've done it, Chuck! Now you're gonna have to stew in your own sorrow!

Revenge is not for me, Chuck. Revenge is better left for others, if you get what I mean. You'll see now that I can still be a friend! I know you're bashful. Most likely you were too shy to show up. I understand. Poor ol' wishy-washy Chuck!

I never know what's going on!

Get off the phone, big
brother. I'm expecting a
call from my sweet baboo!

You know that's not so.
Linus is far, far away. And
anyway, he wouldn't be
calling you.

Incidentally, here's his
latest postcard. Read it. He
mentions you.

P.S. Have I seen any good
movies lately!

I'll sue! That's what I'll do!

Argh!

Hey!

You're back?!!

My dad changed his mind. He didn't like the new job.

What kind of neighborhood is this? It didn't change a bit while we were gone! Don't people ever progress around here? What a stupid neighborhood!

Oh, yeah, she's back too....

Your sweetie is back!